The Endless Unbegun

Also by Rachel Jamison Webster

September
The Blue Grotto

The Endless Unbegun

Rachel Jamison Webster

Twelve Winters Press

Sherman, Illinois

Published by Twelve Winters Press

P. O. Box 414 • Sherman, Illinois 62684-0414 • twelvewinters.com

The Endless Unbegun was first published by Twelve Winters Press in 2015. "*Quiddity* Interview with the Author" appeared in *Quiddity* international literary journal, issue 8.1, and is reprinted with permission.

Cover and interior page design by TWP Design.

Cover art: *Self Portrait as John the Baptist* Copyright © 2012 Lauren Levato Coyne. Used by permission. Visit laurenlevato.com for more information about the artist and her work.

ISBN
978-0-9895151-7-7

Printed in the United States of America

Acknowledgments

Thank you to the editors of the following journals and anthologies who first published some of these poems and prose pieces, some in slightly different forms.

"Wish" in *Passages North*

"Cimbrone"
"Verde"
"Lord"
"The Blue Grotto"
"That Life Was Like a Garment"
"Meanwhile, I Was Floating, I Was Ferried"
in *The Blue Grotto* (a chapbook published by Dancing Girl Press, 2009)

"The Middle Distance" in *I Might Not Tell Everybody, But I Will Tell You: Correspondences with Walt Whitman* (Northwestern University English Department, 2012.)

"The Child Asks" in *A Writer's Congress: Chicago Poets on Barack Obama's Inauguration* (DePaul University Humanities Center and Poetry Institute, 2009)

"Manzanillo" in *On Human Flourishing: An Anthology of Poetry* (McFarland, 2015)

CONTENTS

continued

contents continued

To my parents, Cynthia and Jim Webster

The Endless Unbegun

All those who love and who think, who think and who think about loving, know that there exist during every period a few clandestine beings, born to watch over the little double flame, that it doesn't go out. Sparks in the darkness. Why do you keep watch, while the human tribe sleeps across the earth, indifferent to misfortune, to wars, to joys, to massacres? asks the watcher. There has to be someone, Kafka answers. Watchers, prophets of the present, agents for the most arduous, most dangerous cause there is: to love the other, even before being loved. Without waiting, without counting. The cause of "you."

—Hélène Cixous
Stigmata: Escaping Texts

WHO AM I?

I am the Wish that Jon and Marisol have. And also what watches the wish being wished. And how lovely it is! From here, I can see its shape, hear its perfect note in the endless sound that rings rings in water, which is this.

The rings move both without and within, and the watcher watches from both within and without. And it is this watched equilibrium in motion that they wish for, more than the story that unfolds around it. The story, they know, will begin to feel like clothing, something other people notice. Always, whenever they are living their stories, they are simultaneously outgrowing them, like jackets they will shrug off, because beneath, a new layer of self has grown. This is because Jon and Marisol are lovers, those who with all their longing long for an end to longing.

Their longing has gone on so long they've devised many methods for parceling it out, for keeping it tidy and making it useful. It is, after all, dark outside. It is the early twenty-first century. So both, in their way, read magazines and websites and self-help, and both know that no one can complete you, everyone agrees, and so they pour their longing into objects, and into their work, which is with objects and with words and ideas manipulated like objects. It is a cluttered world, and they love it, because it is where they've learned themselves. They've gathered moss, they've gathered world, they've gathered and cloaked themselves from themselves. But, wait, I'm getting ahead of myself. That was before they met. Before they met, they even turned back to their pasts and gathered love there, in their own earlier selves. Before they met, they tried everything. After they met, they had to try everything else.

When they saw each other for the first time in a bar in Chicago, the dingy room trembled with memory. There you are, Marisol thought, and very soon afterward they were talking. He didn't look the way she'd expected him to. And he didn't know why she looked so familiar, like a sister.

They were almost of equal height, with Marisol in her heels. She was pale, with hazel eyes and an elegance about her due to a certain withholding. If she didn't know you were watching, she would lift into herself, into a kind of lightness, her fingers would flutter, she would almost seem to levitate in her sweater. But watched, knowing herself watched, she'd become solid, she'd try to press herself into her own eyes, to enter the world that way, through her own looking. She was, after all, a beautiful woman, and she was shy and angry about always being watched. She'd been in the cage of others' gaze her whole life. She was longing to be watched from within. So if there was any thrust in her at all, it came through her eyes.

Jon, for his part, longed to be watched from without, but he didn't know this. He'd been holding up others his whole life, and he would have liked to have been beheld. Marisol looked at him, she saw him, she almost looked into him, but he didn't trust her, didn't trust why she kept talking to him. He thought it must be some kind of market research. He thought she was getting something from all of this, something she could sell later as a clever anecdote. Of course he thought this way. Jon was living in this time, as was Marisol, which means they'd been trained primarily in the arts of buying and selling, and we can't go into the despair of all that now.

Jon was not a large man. He did not overeat or overindulge in drink, nor did he indulge in fear. This was, perhaps, the most unusual and gallant thing about Jon. He looked Marisol in the eye. His eyes were a deep brown, maybe the color of coconut wood, and he fiddled with his beer with the most differentiated hands Marisol had ever seen. Not differentiated from one another, of course, but from everyone else's hands. Marisol thought she had never seen such distinct hands. And yet, his body language, his stance, was hesitant. He looked as if he were trying to pull away from an inevitability. And Marisol, for her part, was scaring herself—the way she leaned into him, having never leaned into a situation like this before. Do we know later when we first recognize another?

Both had been in bad relationships. Both had been in good re-
lationships. Both had been free. Both had been tied. Both had
thought the worst possible thing would be to think more about
the one you love than they think about you. Both had thought the
worst possible thing would be to be the one harmed. When they
thought *harm*, they thought being impaled, being maimed, being
disfigured, being crippled, being poisoned, being tubercular, being
pathetic, being annoying, being abandoned, being paralyzed, being
dark, being hackneyed, being a lackey, being a yawn—the list went
on and on.

Afterwards, they left the bar with one another's email addresses,
objects in a world of objects. Jon's was on some box top, a white
card—his handwriting angular, in black pen. Marisol's—the same
black pen, but an airy cursive, a little too neat, he thought, written
on the bottom half of an airport receipt.

Had they not heard the legends? Had no one ever read them
Shakespeare's Sonnet 116—*let me not to the marriage of true minds
admit impediments. Love is not love which alters when it alteration finds?*
When had love become something to be vaguely ashamed of? If
only a poem could have come on the radio! If only a bard at the
end of the bar could have broken into a broken song, a sad Irish
tale about true love.

I would have appeared to Marisol as an older woman crying in the
bathroom over a divorce. I would have delayed her with my crying,
knowing she was compassionate. I would have told her, you know
right away. I would have told her about my love, and would have
made love look a bit unlikely and shopworn so she wouldn't have
known if she'd even really want such a thing. I would have said
that there is a place (which is also a time) in which harm becomes
impossible, because you know that to hurt the other is to hurt the
self. Of course, to say this believably I would have had to change
my diction along with my hair, and, Marisol, if she'd wanted, would

3

have had an odd and funny story out of it.

And to Jon, I would have delivered the most unlikely triple play with the most uncanny timing. And because Marisol was in the bathroom, he would have seen it all, and seeing it, would have known that he'd dreamed this exact play the night before, had dreamed even the woman returning from the bathroom, not apologetic, or catty, not making a nervous joke, but returning to him, taking up their conversation. And he would have faced her open face, about to ask a question.

At times I was beside them, and at times I was above. At times, I was nursing a beer at the end of the bar and fiddling my own worry over how the game would turn out. There was not enough belief in the world, it seemed to me, present-day belief. And where were the lovers, the ones who would hold one another's eyes and simultaneously arrive?

JON

I live in Philly, and I run an antique shop. Well, that's a fancy name for what I do. I have a space on the North side, and I buy out estates and whatnot and then sell the furniture and records and old lady coats and videocassettes and CDs. It's getting hard to sell even CDs these days—I have them marked down to a dollar for five. I bought the space banking on gentrification, and have waited five years for it to happen. I still feel on the crumbling edge of something. I know this is partly because I am attracted to what is crumbling, and partly because "progress" does not move outward in even concentrics. Besides, like most people my age, I don't believe progress is really progress anyway.

The neighborhood is diverse—made up mostly of immigrants, a few squatting students and artists, single mothers and grandmothers raising whole families of children, amazingly hardworking illegals, drunks and junkies. But it feels wrong to describe them this way. I know their names, and I help them out, I guess, by buying their things from them when they need to make rent. Usually they buy the stuff back, at the markup, but sometimes they just can't, and whatever it was—a grandmother's brooch, a TV stand, an old Rolex or violin—gets sold to someone else.

Most of my lots come from the suburbs—old white people who've been given up to death or to nursing homes and whose stuff has been given up by their kids in a single swipe. Maybe their parents lived too long and the goodbye was too drawn out. Maybe none of them really lived. I don't know. Maybe it's just too much for people to return to the past like that, to sift through all the objects their parents held onto. I pay them a flat rate and sometimes I can't believe what they won't bother with. Some guy gets five hundred dollars for his mother's furnishings, and my guys and I go over and fill the truck and all the drawers and cupboards of the furniture are still packed with the family's life. I spend all day going through some woman's drawers, and they are filled with things her son should have wanted—embroidered handkerchiefs and a photo of his father and his own baby teeth tucked into a little handsewn silken pouch. So now I've got a store full of dressers, credenzas and Carol King LPs, and a little rattling handful of some dude's teeth.

Marisol

I traffic in air—advertisements, slogans—and I love working on planes. On this flight, I am working on a new campaign for McDonald's—a way to sell junk food to poor people, I think sadly, and then realize that this thought is a sure sign that I have switched demographics. I grew up on McDonald's. We would get so excited to go to McDonald's as a family, and I can still taste the fries, the faintly metallic cheese and toasted bun of the cheeseburger, the thrill of the single pickle. I can see the drifts of salt I'd dip the collapsing fries into and the grease bleeding through the paper placemat, making it a strange transparent map.

I think if I have kids, I'll make sure to take them to McDonald's once in a while, even though I'll eat organic most of the time. I think it is an integral part of being American somehow. And thus my campaign! In order to sell McDonald's, I sell nostalgia. My idea was to show home-movie style ads, of kids having birthdays, celebrating homeruns at McDonald's—in that jagged film look of early VHS, the colors fuzzed and tilted in a way we associate with nostalgia. I think it is a good idea, and I think the client liked it. The idea is to show a certain demographic—*my* demographic—that they can go home again.

In two years, I will officially switch demographics, and my concerns will change. This seems contrived, but it is also tested and proven. As a woman, I will become more aware of myself biologically, of my clock, as they say, and that will make me more concerned about things like health insurance, and mortgages—and marriage.

It is so strange to have life all mapped out the way I do, and also to see through the map. Sometimes I want to rise out of it altogether, slip into some higher, lighter destiny, not unlike the scene outside my window now. We are above the clouds, and they are drifted and dry-cracked as a desert. We are in another unstrummed layer of air, and it makes me think of currents, movements, how much is really possible. From here, the world's biggest cities look like toys.

JON

"I think a lot about what people are willing to sell, and what they are forced to sell," I told Marisol when I met her. Right after I told her I managed a Pawn Shop. It was a strange thing to say. What a depressing phrase. Who was the pawn?

Isn't a pawn shop just some kind of turnstile of want? And didn't my life have a little more refinement than that? Didn't an antique shop offer something better—the promise of the diamond in the rough, the original print or first edition or Stickley chair that the dealer had overlooked or mismarked and that you could barter into some kind of elegance or freedom? And wasn't I also selling this idea, this opportunity to the one who searches, the one who keeps her eyes open?

"I think all the time about what people are willing to buy," Marisol had answered. "It's my job. I work in advertising."

MARISOL

On this flight, I have my own row, which is even better than first class, where they are too attentive and my dreaming is always intermittent. And, as successful as I am, I suppose I feel a little less like myself in first class.

In the row beside me are three little kids—the oldest, a girl near the window, another girl in the middle, and a little boy on the aisle. The oldest is watching all of them, and is happy for the job. She helps her brother order his drink, she covers their legs with a blanket, and now she is playing dolls with her sister.

She holds two identical dolls with brown bobbed hair, one in each hand. They are naked except for painted-on white underwear, and they have dresses of molded plastic. The dresses snap over their little bodies like coffins. The girls are talking to the dolls, holding them up to their faces and making them speak in soft voices.

My sister and I also played with dolls, but baby dolls, mostly. I remember them—Jennifer and Beth, Brianna and Amy—and the way I could read their thoughts. I took care of them so sincerely, rocking them, dressing them, putting them to sleep, that they became real to me. They watched me and knew me, just as I knew them. Then one day, I could no longer hear their voices, and they started hardening back into plastic. I started thinking of lipgloss instead, and the boys I wanted to watch me. And when I turned thirteen, my mom took me to the mall and bought me a tight pair of designer jeans and, with that, I was launched into the world of products. The mysterious realms were shutting down then, into this realm.

Now the girl reads. She runs her precise brown finger under the words and mouths them with her perfect rosebud lips. Then she looks up and laughs a little like she is sharing a joke with the story.

JON

The sign outside the shop once advertised a local jazz radio personality but now is old and weathered. It's only a few years old, actually, not nearly as old as the building, or the train tracks where commuters drone by every morning, but old enough so that the man's face is peeling away from the wall. First he bubbled up all over, then his cheeks began to scale away like a leper's, then his chin frothed up into a fleeing beard, and now I can see the bricks that were his eyes.

I wonder if I'd know he was a man if I hadn't known he'd once been a man. I look at it every day and think of how, someday, the actual man and his actual flesh will peel away from his actual bones. He'll be as damp and soggy and up against the wall as his photo is now. Poor bastard.

But then again, so will I. While all this furniture surrounding us will mutely endure.

Time, I think, moves more slowly for me than it does for other people. I feel its layers. Maybe that's why I have a hard time doing much, or feeling like I'm doing much. Sometimes I feel fossilized by my own time.

WISH

If I were Jon and Marisol's Wish, they were also mine. Or, to be more precise, my wish was for a book that would be alive, written from the kind of union that capitulates one through death into birth again, into layers of being where life feels more real. I wanted to write it—the way we can enter time like riding a current, the way we can meet others wholly, who then become portals to our fuller becoming.

The first book I ever wrote was for my brother, and I called it "Things that Fly." I was almost three, and nearly half of my life had been spent waiting for him to be born, wondering what he would look like, what his name would be. Finally, he arrived from the other side, and because he did not get out much on this one, I took it upon myself to tell him what he could expect to see in the sky. I chose construction paper in several shades of blue, and on each page, I drew something in the air—a plane, a bird, a cloud. Our mom helped me finish the book with red yarn knots holding the pages together. He was just learning to sit up, and I would crouch beside him and point out the wonders of this world.

Twenty-seven years later, I was still trying to write that book. I was my book's angel-author and I still had no idea how to make it fly. Then I had my first flying dream. I was walking with a friend through the past. We were in long medieval dresses and little ruched caps, strolling down a wooden boardwalk-style street, carrying baskets of eggs. We came to a still, reflective river, stretching onward to the base of a mountain. The water was placid and edgeless—like what is sometimes called an "infinity pool." I set down my basket of eggs, and suddenly I had a large blue book in my hand the width and size of a kickboard. And as if I were a child just learning to swim, I kicked off with the book before me—into the river and up up into air. I flew! And flying was like swimming.

The next morning, I received a package in the mail from a friend—a birthday gift three months late. I opened the envelope and there was the book from my dream. This book was oversized, with a hard blue cover, worn and rounded a bit on the edges, with a binding made of hand-tied red thread. Its cover had been fashioned from an old library book, and its pages were blank. It wasn't a book I could read, but this book that I would have to write.

Vagaries of Fate and Reincarnates of Fortune

If I were not absent,
my fingers would refuse nothing; in the deep well
the prompt hand that wrote this would wash waters,
drag vines and fix shoots in the gardens.

It was splendor to burn my limbs in the kitchen with you.

—Fortunatus to Radegunde, Sixth-Century France

Fortunatus the Traveler

I woke from that dream with a title in mind: *Wishing Cap & the Middle Distance*. The middle distance was what I would have to travel, that space between performance and communication, between my imagined characters and real characters with life in them, between the small rehearsals of love into Love, .

And when I Googled *Wishing Cap*, I learned that the idea of a floppy red topper that you could don to get your wishes is a very old one. It was connected to a fellow named Fortunatus, and when I Googled *Fortunatus*, I saw that he seemed to keep coming back and back, in different versions of his story, living different angles of his soul. And I wondered, was *that* the wish? To live again and again? To return with the soul's full knowing, and then to live as if to remember it?

In the earliest accounts, Fortunatus was one of the first Christians. He traveled with Paul through the desert and helped carry back epistles, two of which became Corinthians I and Corinthians II—which include the Bible's great passages on love.

Later, at the dawning of the Roman Empire, Fortunatus was a musician-poet. He was born around 530 near Treviso in Venetia, and educated in the city of Ravenna, but like all troubadours, he set off from home. Those were turbulent days, but Fortunatus was able to work his way through the empire. He wrote courtly poems commemorating births, weddings, deaths and wars. He gave to his audience wherever he went, winning hearts, winning a place to stay the season, and winning respite from the violence and depravity of the day. Like many troubadours, he used the language of human love and Divine love almost interchangeably, as if to invite the devout into a more active, living faith, and to invite the carnal into something beyond their bodies.

Then Fortunatus traveled to Poitiers, in France, where he was introduced to Radegunde, a queen who had rejected her riches to devote herself to God, establishing a convent for women. He was so impressed by this woman, so intrigued. He knew he was home. And so once Fortunatus found his true home, which was his true love, his name was free to come back as a word in a story. You can almost see the questions moving like clouds over the storytellers' faces . . . How did he survive by way of transformation? How did Fortunatus find the greatest fortune of all?

The next time Fortunatus appears it is in a Germanic myth, and in this myth, he has a wishing cap made of the most delectable red velvet, and all he has to do is put it on and make a wish, and the wish will be his. But Fortunatus, having genuinely loved his equal other, has a rare sense of proportion. He talks to his higher Watcher (through his hat) all the time, and in this way, he is able to bring his right life into being. And yes, he tells us, there is a *right* life. That is, there are levels of rightness, a way to become more or less real, and they all have to do with the wish, how deep a wish it is, and how well it can dovetail with the Wisher who wishes it.

Centuries passed. Fortunatus's story was told many times—around hearths and bonfires, around kitchen tables and in cobbler's rings. It was told in a pamphlet, and in a series of drawings and in a famous opera. It was told so often, in fact, that it began to be told incorrectly.

In the first alteration, Fortunatus had two sons who were jealous of their father's happiness, which they attributed to the strange cap that he sometimes pulled out in the middle of the night when he thought the boys were asleep. So when they reached adolescence, the boys maneuvered to steal the cap and run away. They did, and tried on the cap, and in that moment one grew very weak, while the other cap-wearing brother grew strong and bullying. It was, after all, the hidden wish of each to dominate the other. So their lives became a scuffle for the cap, interspersed with those accomplishments of wealth and fame that are born from competitive hunger.

The next time Fortunatus appears, he is given the sad fate of these sons, and his name, divorced from his story, is given to mean, simply, one who overvalues the things of this world and misses the point. His name is meant to mean Fortune, as in Fortune 500, as if that is the only fortune. By the time we arrive here, to the moment of Jon and Marisol, Fortunatus has been so long misunderstood, he is understood only as a fool.

But once he was alive, and his wishes were neither simple nor material. They tended to find their form in poems. Often he was wishing to be with Radegunde, the one with whom he felt most whole, most known. He kept writing that particular wish: to get back to her.

RADEGUNDE

I exist somewhere between time and eternity. If you look me up you will learn that I was born around 520 to the ruling family of Thuringia, an area in Germany between the Rhine and the Elbe. I was of the royal pagans living at the edge of the Roman Empire. When I was ten, Clotaire, King of the Franks, invaded and killed my family—my mother, uncle, siblings and servants, plundering and burning the wealth of our kingdom. I escaped with one brother because we were the smallest and able to hide. We crouched in a tree, hardly breathing. We watched them have their way with our sister, one after the other, then lance her with their swords. We watched them rape our mother and then slit her neck and kick her body as she lay bleeding. Then we trembled, voiceless, when they came for us. But Clotaire liked the look of me. He treated us as trophies and brought us back to his court. Instead of making us slaves, he educated us in the Roman style, and when I turned thirteen, he made me one of his wives. But by then it was clear to me that my survival and my destiny lay in the world beyond this world.

Clotaire grew to love me, and offered me every material thing, but I ignored my worldly status and kept my eyes fixed on God and the unfolding I felt around and within me. When Clotaire had my one remaining brother killed in 550, I fled him and his kingdom to live as a nun. In time, I requested his support to establish an Abbey in Poitiers, France. He gave this support until his death, and afterward his sons funded my abbey, which served as a respite for devout women, and women who had been given up by their families, dishonored, impregnated, or harmed by the violence of our world. From there, I corresponded with my brothers-in-law and nephews, trying to give them perspective as they participated in the politics and religion of the day, which were inextricable, one and the same. I was friends with bishops, queens, kings and princes, including Gregory of Tours. My dearest friend was Venantius Fortunatus, a troubadour who wrote many letters and poems to me and who composed my biography after my death.

That is my story. I contact the writer, who represents one aspect of my Wish—although that wish seems implanted in me by her wishing!—with little bits of my memory. They are single scenes, little Byzantine mosaics. And even as she writes them, she wonders if what she needs is more faith, or less. Would it all flow more easily if she really believed the idea that she is, in fact, me—a portion of my soul, that is, which is to say a reflective shard of the universal soul we all share? Or would it be easier if she could just take it all a bit more lightly—it is just a story, after all, and stories are never true. Even true stories are artifice. But going this route is tedious and nihilistic, is it not? What is the point of telling an untrue story to which we have no mysterious connection? To convey some moral? To prove the finer points of our artifice? To make something to sell, to entertain?

There are plenty of things to do these days that are more entertaining than reading, but few that are more satisfying. A person reads or writes to find a message expressly for them, a character who is, in fact, them, or who could be, by being so other that she expands the self by communion. We read and write to discover ourselves. The same reason we live.

The whole point of all this, I tell her, is to live the little Byzantine mosaics and then slip out of them, peer back into their scenes to feel the space between self and other where the self becomes the other, like someone you fondly remember. Enough of that and you can even slip the space between time and eternity, like wading into a river that shimmers with recognition, in which the visible world is a mirroring of the propulsion which is its becoming. In our time, this margin between life and eternity was called purgatory. It was a stage in the development of the mind—the mind unfolding in a fold, so to speak. The binary of heaven and hell was simply not complex enough—not if people were going to drop their ties to sacred nature and believe all this. We needed something more gradual—a shore to an underworld like Persephone's winter, where we could still communicate with the dead, and where the dead, in turn, communicated with us and carried the memory of life. We needed those channels to speak to our ancestors and unborn—the angels among us.

I had neither ancestors nor children, so I was left with the Word. And I learned that it is the poet's job to wade deep into this margin, to find words for the mergers that tip the mind with recognition and make the body feel like it is swimming with stars.

A Note on the Form

Dreaming, we drop into conglomerations of faces.

Researchers surmise the dream, even epic,
transpires in only a moment and is not
to our sleeping minds a story
siphoned out over time
but a lit diorama, a revelation,
that proceeds as our eyes
troll the folds of our lids.

We dreamers are the angels
added late to the frame
of a medieval painting.

We look down naked into selves
and faces and say, I was that one, this
happened to me.

Radegunde: Illuminated

I was rescued from the forest by fate
in its dark cape and hair-covered hands.

They were men's hands, heavy with rings,
and they turned me
to look at me—my body

bow-thin and singing, my face
pattered with green light
dripped from the tongues of trees.

That was after they'd slashed my mother's lap
and the lap of the land
had caught

my brother and me
in its thicket of smells, a dampness
I knew as grief.

Hiding, our hearts beat, wracked
by what we'd seen:
       head-thump onto wood, eyes wild
       for the severed body, the blood-tide.

       Bones snapping under axes, breaking
       like branches, like shelter for what
       through them was passing—

The cold climbed our teeth
and we watched
darkness sift into the world

through a sky of the strangest color—
something stirred of egg and indigo
and brushed behind the trees in a book.

Night froze black the branches,
then sifted down to us
as dust, making dust
of our shoulders and arms,

breaking into our faces,
until even the silver limn
of cheekbone was gone,

until he and I were just
quick liquid guidings of the eye.

That was how they found us,
thinned with shivering,
blood and rubble in our hair.

That was how they saved us
from what they'd done to us.

They tipped their skins to our lips,
giving us pannikin, water and bread
that broke to a powder on my tongue.

Then the muscles of their horses
moved under us, every shoulder-pull
grinding me deeper into time.

That night, I knew
I'd be wedded to darkness.

I'd have to take it in to my body.

SPOILS

In the main hall, as plunder,
I was washed and dressed
in fine embroidered cloth.

My hands hung useless
in the stone-cold air
as they pulled back my hair and combed for nits
then braided it with vermillion
ribbons the handmaid had dyed.

> (While my mother was bleeding out
> into dirt, she was seeing color seep the silk
> and sleepy, thinking, this is the sun, the sun
> seeps into me, it seeps into my son through me . . .
>
> She'd let her boy suck the color from her thumbs
> that night, all her milk gone
> and her nipples split by the gums of princes,
> she'd rocked and hummed against his hunger.)

I was lost in that paddle clack and strange
language, cold corridors where I
abandoned my eyes
and sought the shades, some forgiveness
from my kin for living.
And none came.

I had watched my mother like the waters
recede from the earth, and I knew God
was not simple or starved as a man,
was not *Lord*, as they said,
in creweled nobleman's robes. No,

better to call God nothing
but breath moving through the barn of bones.

Better to be patient, trace
knowing's face with hands my own.

SOON

I was a girl when he took me,
roughing me to enter,
and I looked into his eyes every time.

It wasn't long before he was afraid
of the still places I could go in my body.
Soon, he overlooked me more
for the others, though he knew

I was given to rapture, to kneeling
in barns praying until my knees and flattened
feet split skin. In the haylight,
sun spinning spores and glittering dust,
I became those long blond fingers
crossing and recrossing themselves.

I was hollow as straw
and holy gold, rising
not knowing who I had been before,
little flicker winging out
into stars and hands,
and works of hands.

CANDLING

Candling, my life was
candling me, a luminous wand
dipping, dripping with an inward light,
gathering gradually around the thin twisted
string I was. Sleepless, I was sleeping, dipping
candles to light by the light of the candles,
my brow beading oil, my face burning over
the burning bowl of the thing diminishing
to yield up what was gathering. That vat of wax
was the sun in earth's gut and my wicks were dunn
doves diving its broth, drawing out
the slickening shrouds, like acts
receding in a film, like days
accruing over others, slipping
from their skins, and thickening
to the mass that bodies the burn.

Knot of Power

Everything they gave me I gave away that was my way
of not belonging to them. I slipped the knot
of that kind of power and knew it
as just a twist of matter, nothing
that would not burn.

In that long dry penance
of wealth, I did not tire
of surprising servants
I'd decided were deserving—
with a ruby ring or slips embroidered in gold.

Art and the commerce of the world.
Counterfeits of power was all they were
and even a milking girl knew
that the jewel pinned deep in her bodice
could deliver her from the bloodknot
the nobleman had planted in her and did not want.

I'd sit at the table, mute or boring
the other wives with lieder or liturgy,
then when they'd left to their toilette,
I'd stuff crusts and plums, boiled eggs,
little pewter pitchers of milk
into my cloak, into the folds I'd sewn.

In this way, I slipped from my station
and entered my life. Disguised
by plainness of intention, I fed the poor
and mixed tinctures of herbs,
planted gardens, administered cures.

I liked to see the closing of a wound.
I liked to see an undocked eye anchoring
for a time on human kindness.

I did not aspire to be good,
but truth was in me like a hunger.

It devoured the surrounding lies
and left me with a seed
to tend, my Love a little leafing.

JAR

Clotaire returned from his latest conquest
angry, haunted by the deeds he'd done.

He'd had my dove-brother killed.
He would have fallen had he tried himself.
He was weak as only the rich can be.

> My brother! Who never gave a hard word,
> struck down in his first blond beard
> by my own husband!

Worse than being murdered myself
to know he was gone. My own little human
life meant nothing now to me.

Let me go, I said, despising
at that moment the stinking Lord
and all the exploits of men as a clay jar
shattered from the shelf, the holy ghost
assisting me in my moment of need
or was it his terror clattering at the walls?

In time, I demanded the property in Poitiers
knowing my own home was over.

His fear of me gave me leave.
And from there, we built a life
from his respect for me, and my nullity.

REGRET GALLOP

Why was my brother ripped from the world
by men of little faith?

Why did I flee, having twice
endured the enemy?

I did not attend his funeral.
I did not kiss close his eyes

nor let hot tears drop
to warm the unlucky corpse
inside of me.

Life was denied.
I might have sent the fringes
I made to his bier!

With him went my joy.

Sister

My bloodline ended as the spirit
claimed me, webbing
me out into world
not as body but word embodied—

writing letters to bishops and princes,
raising others' daughters, plums
and herbs from Love and some cool air
of my tending.

The Endiing's Enclosed in the Beginning

So much food all at once;
at first I welcome it—
meats, vegetables, filling the silver bowls.

I swear, greens float in a fat sauce
like twigs in the sea foam;
these dishes seem like an entire garden!

A glass platter is passed around
with plump chickens, their wings trussed up.

Many chefs have decorated baskets
of fruit, tempting, gorging me with odors.

From a black jar I pour
milk into a white cup.

—Fortunatus to Radegunde, Sixth-Century France

CIMBRONE

The ending's enclosed in the beginning.
The tree's death uncurls its seed.
Once, as another, I loved you,

and we walked through the garden, through
hedgerows and hollies, prehistoric aloes,
lemon trees in glossy copses, arbors dripping wisteria.

All this was called a honeymoon.
All this was surrounding a stone manor house
mortared to a ridge.

Below us, the sea broke itself open
on rocks. It thrust and foamed up
toward terraces furred with olives,

arthritic tomatoes, aubergines
and shrubby plums. And above all this
staked, robust fecundity, we walked

so slowly we hardly seemed to be walking,
between terra cotta bowls of wax,
their lit wicks flicking little gold fish

against our ankles, and up the drifts
of my skirt. We walked among the statues
of saints who had lost their hands to wars

and to wind. We still had our hands,
and we remembered them then
and held them along that path

that rimmed the cliff and came
to the Terrazzo dell'Infinito—a quiver
where sky becomes water and water, sky.

We walked as if we knew that stage
would hold us, though we did not know
it would hold us, and the blue

surrounding was deeper and wilder
than my comprehension of blue,
and I did it, and I do,

pull back and back through
until I see us: two small bodies, mute
flecks of foam on the lip of the species-wave,

squinting into future and saltspray.
We stood there, rot-eyed as the stone
sentinels lined up around us.

Once, they had seemed so real,
their semblance had protected
against all advances,

but sea-storms and years
of staring isolately outward
had worn them slowly down to these—

moss-spackled faces, flat heads
shy and backlooking as books.

VERDE

Then someone showed us to a room.

It had a carved walnut writing desk
topped with a pewter bowl of fogged plums,
green and white Spanish tile,
and an orange wing chair
spangled with bright birds.

I put on a long blue linen dress.
I kept trying to decide between
a cardigan or shawl.

I looked long in the long mirror,
trying to see myself in that room
I had chosen as my life.

I chose the shawl.
I chose the necklace of turquoise and gold.
I chose the copper-colored slippers.

It was the first year of the twenty-first century.
At last, I have entered my present,
I thought, but it was the past.

LORD

But you wanted to be no one's guest.
You wanted the patron's room over the sea,
the one slung on the jaws of infinity.

You decided the room they gave us
called verde, the garden room,
the genius room,
was not the right room for me.

So you pressured and paid
for that wider berth
haunted by commerce.

Doors opened there too,
then slammed and shuttered us
in the host's disapproval.

Storms blew wide the windows
and long knots of hair
appeared in the bath.

And in that new room,
away from the green and slow-opening
door, I drank and I fucked
you so hard you felt used.

My present was my past
and my future was coming at me
in dreams: an old man

pushing a shopping cart
filled with turpentine, rags,
hubcaps and smashed cans.

What was for sale was everything he had,
alley after alley he was after me, no end
to what he'd sell for parts.

THE BLUE GROTTO

Their eyes were the surface
of a sea so oil-trafficked
I would not swim.

It filled and slid
over the old stone formations,
magma that erupted up once
then cooled

into carbuncles, nodes and tonsils,
knuckled spires, sweeps
of hip and clavicle.

What were they
to make of earth
this profligate and hot?

They sold it off in tours,
made each shape a caricature,
named them Dolly Parton,
Elvis's Guitar, Colossal Shotgun
and the Taj Mahal.

Some Gaping Terror
they named the earth.

FORTUNATUS SINGS

Beware the modern pawnshop
is sterile and armored.

It is slick and efficient as an online sale.
It feels almost like an honor to sell yourself there.
It feels almost like a bank or a spa, almost like a luxury
to give yourself away.

Beware the modern pawnshop is a pawnshop.
Beware the modern pawnshop is a cul-de-sac of wishes.
Beware the world's a pawnshop, a pawnshop,
a cul-de-sac of wishes. Beware the world, beware the wish,
beware the wish the world is wishing.

Once We Were Inside Time

I see everything at once flowing past like a river of air.

But of you I see nothing.
And all other things are not enough to satisfy me.

—Fortunatus to Radegunde, Sixth-Century France

LUCE

I tried to leave the world.
And I did, for a time.
They are right—it is heaven
looking down like that.

From that distance, it isn't life
stripped clean as bone
but a vast tapestry softened
by atmosphere, by intervening breath.

I could see it was not all equal.
There were threads more vivid
than others, more essential
to the central design.

I was complicit,
but it was not my design.
Words spilled from my tongue.
Anyone I wanted to be
I already was.

Then, what was it—
ambition? or love—
made me enter again
the one body.

Never mind it was all
based on an irony,
having seen it
from the end like I had.

I had been praying to fate
so long, I recognized the fates
even when I did not choose them.

Any early glee in that
fell away like bright dry leaves.

I knew I had been chosen
to live out this particular failure.

THAT LIFE WAS LIKE A GARMENT

I shuddered before its clutter and dust,
before the stuffed armoires
and all the costumes of hiding.

Photos of me at every age, those ribbons
they pin on beauty queens and goats at fairs.
Shells in bowls, rose petals and veined stones.

The past in corsets and boned hats.
The past in these pages, their names
flaking off like skin. The past in the rape
and long wooded confusion out of that.

And on one wall, a painting of a horse,
running, its muscles foamed
with faint shores of sweat.

On the other, a window,
framed in wood, knotted
with words rooted in the ringing years.

And through that window is the future.
And the future is a field—
the same field
where the horse of the memory runs,
the same horse.

And no one owns the field.
And we are there, the sky unwinding
over and inside us like woodflesh.

THE TURNSTILE OF THE HESITANTS

For so long I was circling
at the turnstile of the hesitants.

That metal bar kept punching me
in the stomach—every time a surprise—
while behind me, guys
were selling concessions.

Then I heard you calling,
*Hurry, someone you know
is about to take the field—*
and it was me—far below,
and all of us in our human forms,
playing out our human lifetimes.

I had never been as happy
as I was there with you
in your washed blue shirt,
your hands open patiently
on your own knees,
beside me and simultaneously
long below in motion.

We watched so long
my circling at the turnstile
became a kind of preparation,
a learning to read the air,
the way we once read the shoals of time
from eternity's deeps.

I waited so long to spin
into my brown body, it became
a bit absurd—the idea of a body!
Remember, I said, years later,
before we were born?

We were up in a lookout
holding a bowl carved from bone,
and we watched the people
move out over the land.

We saw ourselves passing
as any species passes—
hungry, burnt and thirsty
as she was, the earth.

THE TOWER

I was up in a tower of my mind, spinning
the hours' wheel, the days' wheel,
then with a needle, I pricked my finger
and the one bead of blood drumming up
became the ruby I could sell for my freedom.

I pressed it like a purchase to a child's lip.
I pressed it into a burnished rosette
in this big blank book.
Freedom, for what? I thought.
It's life I want.

I stepped into my days,
and they wanted me, they spun me
like a confection in their gaze.
I stepped into the city
and it shined, glossy with desire,
slick as love's thighs,
sticky as the flower's split stem.

Until living, until giving,
I grew tired again
and returned to my tower, my fear
of the watch-hers who were not me,
with their transmissions
and trust funds and teeth.

I wanted only my wooden rocking spindle,
my certain chores and little window
on the sleepy street.

I wanted only to become
my own Watcher.

And finally, I did.
She was silent and dark.
She'd existed before
language, before love,
in a warm and roiling swamp.

I rested as her for a thousand years.
I rested as a backbone cradled in stone.
And eventually, from that fossil, I rose
into something thin as a gesture,
a slight glimmer in light.

Time and again,
Orpheus carried me like that,
as if I were his charm.

I think it was me, the swing of my arm,
or my hand brushing hair from my brow.
In any case, you know
how he sang of it, as if loss
were the only poem.

As if I were bent wrist
or bowed lips or any part
widowed from the ocean I Am.

QUILL

Now anything I make is from
my own within, my own beginning.

At first I am a fin, a flipper then a feather-
spine gradually widening into branch, distending
into limb then finger, lush flowing of the blood
into folios of gills and the ear's little sea anemone—

And any God there is is watching in wonder,
mouth open in wonder and I am
that mouth, opening in wonder.
There where you are too.

Once We Were Inside Time

You moved first
through the eye-ring, drowning
in air and battered then
by matter's mad stewards.

And one day, we'll slip out again,
and all this will have been
a single, evaporative breath.

I watch the waters now
for the floating ring of your eye.
I know the slow coal of the pupil,
the stone before the watering
and the kiss that opened you
into a body.

I was there in the moment
of the two in two in one
that became you.

I was not even the beginning
of a body then, not even
the yellow of first light,
but I was there,
in the beyond-white.

AS THE WATERS DIVIDED

From what place do you—radiating with light—
return to me? What delays held you?

My joy you took away with your departure
you deliver back with your homecoming.

—Fortunatus to Radegunde, Sixth-Century France

Have We Met Before?

Did I once reach across and take your hand?

And did our eyes meet then
as if coming upon the first mystery—

that pond in the woods, nearly hidden
by bramble and wild cabbage?

Remember the planked bridge
and books burned open on the rim?

Remember how we arrived
in that stare, in the still dark water

where the past is the future
and one is the other?

Life Is Just One Long Forgetting, I Said

As infants we pull our first breath—
red thread fraying wild at the eye—

and breathe on in a kind of
onward rocking shedding.

But you called life a recollection
of the light that composed us to matter.

Forgetting, remembering,
we have only the space between.

We are alive. That means
we have more to ask with these bodies.

For Years

For years, you sat in the filthing city, waiting
for your life to begin.

You waited at kitchen tables,
on ballfields, in backseats, in boredom's low drone.

Then you discovered your own hands
could craft things from small sticks:
a deer, a bird, a slight canoe.

And you thought you saw your own form
coming closer, a bundle of kindling
silhouetted in streetglow.

You thought then
you'd recognize your life.

You'd walk toward it
walking toward you.

MEANWHILE, I WAS FLOATING, I WAS FERRIED

My dad owned the boat and I owned the prow.
I arced off the front like the carved maidenhead
as the waters divided around us
in white-furred furious paws,
while inside me, life
was weaving its red nest.

Sometimes when we anchored—
the radio tinnily on, our mouths
working salted chips and peanuts,
I could see it—a dark mark
further off, a circle
I knew held a child.

I thought she was.
I thought she was my sister.
I thought she was my girl.

And I pointed the way to her.
Faster! I'd call back to my dad,
leaning forward then, toward her
waiting, her rescue.

How many days did I dream her—
afternoons into evenings
that settled their pink gauze
along our shoulders and arms
as the ripples silvered, the sky silvered
and the horizon thinned
into only the memory of separation.

Is that what we wanted,
to come upon life that way,
on the horizon, always
on the horizon, like the surprise

we had expected all along,
almost as if we'd crafted it
with our own hands
or fished it from the milkdream of being?

Is that what we wanted: to be
the vessel and clear braid
of our wake.

BOATYARD

Now I climb into your voice like a boat
and it holds me as waves
bell and chuckle at the prow.

Do you remember when we were young
and still keeping track of our rebellions?
Remember, we broke into that boatyard in winter?

I wanted you to find me beautiful and exciting,
so of course I never told you
I found you beautiful and exciting.

I took secret snapshots of you for my little room,
which was already cluttered as anyone's
who's trying to reinvent the garden.

We were teenagers, glossed souvenirs
of a life we lived once
when we were teenagers.

We hadn't seen far into one another's eyes.
We'd seen mainly the smooth planes of our faces,
winter light smacking them like metal.

Our boat was cold white fiberglass
forked up on trusses.
We unsnapped the tarp
and climbed in and into its dark.

We laid back in hollow bodies,
on benches slung over
the hollow belly of the boat.

My hands grabbed your cold buckle,
and we knew our story then and we wanted it
over.

From here, I can hear our laughter,
chill, serrated. Beer caps
thrown hard and fast against a hull.

CELL

The first time we talk, we tell stories like this.
The second time we talk, we talk about form,
which we are always outgrowing.

I tell you my life is as ill-fitting
as someone else's shirt.

It is midnight and I am wading
through my garden—around
beleaguered mounds of sage,
chives and drying weeds
tendrilling into one another,
in silvered halftones, as if waiting
to split again into color,
like waiting for time
to catch up with eternity.

THE MIDDLE DISTANCE

Dear Radegunde,

Everywhere the tightening ice, the brittle hoarfrost,
the pliant grassblades are beaten down.

The trees carry soft snow on their highest leaves.

The thickening river wears a heavy skin,
its weight chaffing the waters, the currents frozen.

In the middle of the river a crystal iceberg floats:

We do not want to go under—or over!
Who can find passage through this battling water?

—Fortunatus to Radegunde, Sixth-Century France

BARDO

All night I am ferried in a boat
by my pregnant friend.

The water is deep, the night
velvet and deep.

She steers us expertly,
past diminutive white cities,
through archipelagos of blue and green.

Then she delivers me
to the other side, where I have a child
who wants to wear a necklace
strung of beads of blood.

Is this the bardo, the ocean,
the expanse between death
and the unbegun? the child asks.

I cannot answer, I am trying
to tie the strands but I am unfamiliar
with the animals of my hands.

I try again and fail a knot,
and fail a knot again,
when you call, waking me
to the ring and the wand
of your voice.

It wants to steer me, shield me,
from the wilderness of sleep,
of me.

Undifferentiated liquid, it breathes
both within me and outside me, heavily
as a sea.

I listen amid the clock's tick,
counterfeit drum
of what the blood does.

THE MIDDLE DISTANCE

A child, conceiving of himself
before he's been conceived, asks,
What is the middle distance?

The space before your name, I answer.
The space that between us remains.

The wish of me?
No, the You of you.
Who is the You of me?

The little God we call the future.

What is the middle distance?
the child asks again.

Oceans and plains, mountains and their crossings.
The atmospheric divide between the world
and the world in which it recalls itself
as meaning. All these signals
cross-hatching the air! Layers
of information you will ply,
threading always higher, wider . . .

What else? he asks then, coming closer.
It's any desert you'll have to cross when you arrive
here, in your life.

It is your long highway over land
sculpted by a longing
to be what it was when it was water.

It is your body, which will stun you
with its beauty, with the way it changes
shape and shines. And the metaphor
of the body, which will surprise you
with becoming—avocado in the mouth,
blossom on a branch,
the stinging grass and oiled knee.

It is the metaphor of self,
which will inure you with innumerable faces,
and the self itself, which will
elude you like the name
you know you know.

What else? the child asks then.
It is the past of your future, your early arrival
in cities—thirsty and sleep-deprived
but bitingly alive—in which
you will know yourself
in your aloneness.

And it is this aloneness,
which you will find
like a bloodrooted tooth
in the bread of every one of your loves.

Even this love? the child asks then, frightened.
Yes, even this one, I have to answer.

And at this the child is silent, dissolving
back to water and salt.

I Chose the World, I Went on

I stepped in, but the world
like its atmosphere had worn itself thin
with giving. Still, I took it in,
until it became the word, world
of my own ringed throat, world
of the word glimmering and changing
me in its gaze, and in this way,
the world became a mirrored terrain.

Reflecting panes, they
moved among us—I was not alone—
like tides, they sang back all the notes
of light, and when we lifted them,
like mica, like stones sliced transparent,
they became these pages, backs blank
and faces capturing some of the minglings—
and in this way, they became a kind of change.

I passed through my own eyes.
I walked far through their brown forests
as again and again we pass through
the world through the seam in the world
called meaning, where everything is light
and matter is just an agreed-upon measure,
a collective faith that a thing
is a thing and is real.

As my hand passing over your chest
becomes the wind stirring and rearranging
the grass, as I turn into you
and our faces become others
breaking on the waters.

STOWAWAY

That night I talked you back
to the ropes in your hands,
we had been drinking bad wine
in a vaguely French café
with secondhand decorations
and a plywood sign on a busy road
just outside of neighborhoods and time,
and I said, well, if I were a ghost,
this is definitely somewhere
I would hang out.

You nodded and we walked
to the cold car and kissed until a knock
and a face floating at the window
waved with my red wallet.
How had he known where we were?
Who had he been once
when we were all others?

He looked through air filmed
with snow and smog like a sea,
like some kind of aiding shipmate
committing one of the little rescues
of everyday, threaded by the tar-
covered tug of reciprocity.

CHALLAH

On the the shore we walked over
sand-pocked snow and you
buttoned me into your coat.

I looked up into your face
that was cold and straining thin,
your beard and ears reddening,
and I thought, here you are again,
my rabbi. But you were never
happy then, not with me.

You felt yourself carrying us all
in your thin arms
when all you wanted was
to bend over the holy books
and feel the old wind core
your bones as you glanced
at the candle's ever-changing dance.

You thought that flame alone
could show you more about truth
than our life with all its children
and dirty clothes. Was I the same?
I think so. But your wife
had to rise early, find meaning
in the braid of bread
like the children's soft flesh,
a yeast expanding, and her
kneading it all up into shape.

She was so angry it burnt
to worry about the oil
you were using to read late
and the hunger rubbing ulcers
in the children's stomachs
and the black birds darting
in her eyes and her mumbling
when she washed the cloth
with her chapped hands
infuriated you into a repeating
gesture at the back of your eyes:

snapping her thin wrists
like black branches.
You were the man
and strong enough to
do it, stuff her mouth
with her own broken hands
and she'd have to eat around their gristle
like birds. You never did it,
that was your victory.

You did not touch her.
You all stayed in the dim
house, through years that
seemed a single day, a little overcast,
the starlings rearranging
their glyphs overhead,
but who noticed what
the sky was saying?

You were devoting your face
to the book, moving your mouth
around the saving words,
your black back a bough
bowing low under snow.

They loved you, you know.

MONK

What you loved most was God
in the form of light entering
the shapes of your room, angles
making shadows that lengthened
and thinned so gradually
you knew you'd never tire of it,
the way the real keeps adjusting
its edges, needing nothing
from you but to see it as infinite
tones and not just as poles
of darkness or light.

And from that, you learned
to love your shy hands
washing the one wooden bowl
innocent past thoughts of innocence,
the way your palm cupped clear water
then released in a stream all it had
held that had healed it.

I have come far enough now
to even love the peacock
with his strut! you thought once,
that widening fan of eyes
that claim to be watching
when they only mean to attract.

You stared into their glow
until you knew them from the ocean,
or the humming around the moon,
thought you remembered them
from some other realm
before you remembered
it was all for mating and that
made your face burn
and embarrassed you.

MANZANILLO

If we didn't want to leave our old lives,
why did we find one another?

We can't stay in this house forever,
even with its rosewood balconies,
lights humming with bugs
and dolphins carved into the eaves,
each fin opening
to some bright and living green.

Can you feel us falling up
into stars, those mineral flowers
that burn with their becoming?

I drove us further
than you thought we could go,
and at the low stone bridge
we laughed to see two slow horses
ambling into the road.

We waited for those old bodies to pass
and pulled our car sputtering onto
the mud-rutted road.

There were candles,
shining glasses and our own table
set back amid the leaves.

I was happy and afraid
you hadn't lived long enough
to know what happy means,
what about it has to do with choice
and what is choosing as it's
choosing you.

Life with you is something new.
And we can hardly see
in these wet leaves,
eating the good food
we've been given to eat.

WE PLOD ON IN DARKNESS, WE PLOD ON IN LIGHT

Dear Radegunde,

All men change, as they live through innumerable events; life goes forward with uncertain steps; our minds are confused, anxious about the future, we don't know what daylight will bring.

Leaving again, I was driven by wave and rainstorm in a little boat, through many perils, as the fierce North Wind churned up the river, and the cresting billows curled dangerously. The riverbanks could not hold the roaring waters, and they poured out over the new-plowed fields. Pastureland, countryside, groves, cornfields, trees and willow thickets, all pillaged by an angry mob.

Pity me! In the heavy chop, the rushing torrents, through the blowing terror of wintry blasts, the stern of the boat rose up, the bow fell in the waves, on their watery peaks as on a mountain road; the boat was suspended in gloom.

First the sailor is outlined against the clouds, then, as the wave drops, he is back at field-level. As the storm roils the dangerous river, the prow is swamped by the fast-rising rapids, water rushes against the keel, foe to any peace. We are crushed in a threatening grip.

I don't have time to tell you here all my complaints. I will hold them in my heart to tell you later. May God's special power grant me the happiness of seeing you again.

—Fortunatus, Sixth-Century France

WE PLOD ON IN DARKNESS, WE PLOD ON IN LIGHT

Once, we were ferried into the crook of night.
Water silvered under stars and rocked us in its salt.
There were sixty of us or so, packed shoulder to shoulder
on an open wooden boat. Night capped its cold
on the crowns of our heads and the tips of our ears

and the smallest brothers crawled toward the laps
of the older girls, the few sisters who'd come,
who'd had to leave their mothers
to take care of the men like little wives.

In that dark we could see the faint silvered shapes
of cheekbones and foreheads, sloping shoulders.
We could see the way the girls yielded
when the boys leaned against them,
and the way the fathers sat straight, facing the future
like they faced the blank and broken ocean.

We were locked in the earth's churning,
rocked in the unremitting waternoise of night,
and our bodies pulled into themselves
and seemed to grow smaller, but more solid,
in their groundless, necessary trust—
in the ocean, the boatman, in some tether
to life within a life interrupted forever by war and escape.

For days we huddled like that and did not see land.
We lived the long thirsting hour of the sun
and the slow freezing hour of the night.
We lived in our shells of shy, necessary bravery
and in our hope—a shared tremor of faith,
like a held note stretched out over the waters
of unparted sea and sky in that unnamable color.

We sat, slumped and weary with our dry tack
and powdery bars of protein, and we moved
into it, obediently—into our species' future.

Then we felt our fathers' bodies stiffen on alert
beside us, and we saw—we had passed through
the middle distance and life was taking shape
on the horizon, in a faint bolt of blue.

Mutual recognition. Talk and conjecture
of what it would be like when we arrived.
Survived. We couldn't know then
it would be years, lifetimes before
we'd see them again—the mothers,
grandmothers, sisters we'd left behind.

Some we would never see. And those we would
we'd meet as strangers, in exiled cities
of steel and glass. Their faces would wear
their former faces beneath them
like shadows pitched from hillocks of bone
and old and young, terror and hope
would wrestle there on their surfaces.

But then, that future was behind us
as promise gathered form. We would dock,
there would be beds and pots of hot food,
and time at last beyond war, beyond time,
in the endless sigh of waves and song.

RECEDING

Where have you been? the child asks.

I've been in the latticed hour.

Enough poetry! the child says then.
We no longer have so much time.

Besides, that's not poetry,
but only language pretending to be poetry.

I know, I say, pleased that the future
knows more than I, but sorry
that I have made it feel lonely.

I was in the past, an hour I no longer inhabit.
I was trying to resurrect it prettily.
Was it really so beautiful?
Or did it become beautiful once you lost it?

It was beautiful at the time,
made more so because even as I was in it
I could feel it receding.

Just as the more I approach you,
the more you feel me disappearing?

AGAINST THE BLUE

So it seemed the child was growing old
before he had even been born.

How much of his life would he need to see,
I wondered, before he could believe
life is real, and believing, find a way?

And would I be able to guide him—
through darkness as well as through light?

I was asking myself these questions,
not knowing he was listening, when he said,
Yes, please tell me about the dark.

I have tried, but I have not been accurate
about the fear, so I will try again.

The dark has to do with powerlessness.

Do I have power?
Yes, more than you know.
Yet you will in your life be stunned
by your own powerlessness.

You may be powerless before memories
that may populate you with griefs.

Or worse—you may find yourself powerless
before others. You may look into eyes
and see the human has been switched off there,
like a light. And that is terror.

What will I do? the child asked.
You may choose to call on God.
Or you may feel that God
only enlarges your questions.

I hope you will have the courage to be powerless,
at least once, before Love,
which will lead you to your life.

When you do, you will sense your own shape
silhouetted against the blue,
and your body from that distance
will seem to you a miracle

and your life will be a single,
fragile hour you will enter
as it enters you.

But will I feel myself an accident?
No! How could you be an accident
when you have been forming in sound
throughout this long hour?
How could you be an accident
after your intricate evolution in the womb,
your long climb up the spine?

Now I am just breaking from the wound silk of time,
and it is damp and it is sticky,
but when I arrive, you know I will have forgotten
all this waiting and watching, all this talking.

True. Except in the deep leafbed of your sleep.
You must always remember to sleep.
And know that the rolling beat of your own heart
and the waves of your breath,
their steady measure, are your portion of eternity.

You really have a way of looking at things.
Yes, and it will not be your way.
Your way will be braver.
You will do less skidding off the chasm.

What chasm? the child asked then.

MORIAH

For years then, there was this silence between us.
I used this time to think about sacrifice.

Forever and forever, she wades out into that water.
She lets the water thread and thrum
into her, until the cold prods her womb
and throttles her spine
and the water breaks her at once
into death, into life.

She has been torn into her joy.
She can look it in the eyes.
But for the father, there is something too bright
to face in the child's face.

He's the type who likes to take his knife
to the fat of his mind.
Even when he's had nothing—
no wealth, no rightful heir—he's had that
work of clarity—his thoughts
like cold stones shining up
from the riverfloor.

(But when had love become part of the fat?
Because love had writhed out purpling
his wife's white thighs? Because blood?)
Or was it just that he wanted this,
with a wanting so common
and fragile it terrified him,
who had been strong
and unwanting as God.

She waded out to do the washing.
She waded out in her exhausted body
and saw him walk the child toward the stone
as if he meant to teach him something.

He stood with the child in the center
of their land, land that soon
would be bald with the heap of him,
would sift his flesh as it blackened and slipped
from his bones, his bones that soon
would not even ruffle the grass.

They stood like that, on the peak
of the story. And she left the river and watched
in panic and without surprise
as he wrestled it. The knife
that voice in him that would not quiet.

He tied the child to the rock.
He slid the blade from its sheath
as she roared out into air
that swallowed her sound.

She had carried the child and that
was the miracle: being a body.
Now she was part of the mind
that watches the other part that kills
what it has most desired.

And this watching—it snagged back
the hand—the watcher being watched saw
himself seen by her, saw terror
in the eyes of the offering,
and this triangle of sight
thundered the mind.

He fumbled his way
through the knots he'd made,
and the child saw his father's confusion
like the confusion of the twine,
and he reached up to help his father.

They freed the child's hands
which, like all hands, would have to find,
and set down, their own knives.

Why Did We So Love the World?

The child asked at last, as if the world
had existed long ago.

We loved it for its textures and song.
We loved it for the desert's endless marriage
of rock and wind. We loved it
for marginal marshes and lush jungles.

We loved the smooth plains of a stranger's face.
The way a person's cheekbones could hold ores of grief
or a brow could hinge open in hope.

We loved crackling power lines—
copper and steel spun thin—
and bright billboards, and the marvelous machinery
of the knee and the knuckle.

And we loved anything woven—
rag rugs and woolen throws and fine silks.
And we loved anything growing,
which we planted and pruned and put in our mouths,
which we dried, then watched unbuckling
in water—in teas and dyes, flavors and colors.
We loved the tastes of coffee, chocolate,
chewy rice and the gold serum of an egg,
and the way a taste could bloom and hotten the tongue.

I know! interrupted the child. *All that is the world.*
You are always wooing me with the world.
But how did we so learn to love the world?

Oh, I answered. We loved it
because we loved each other.

Because our love of the world
was finally at last proportional
to our love of one another.

CUPS AND HOOKS

Once I loved the world more
than I loved my other. I populated
our large house with objects
and became like an object among the objects.

There were books lined upright on the shelves
and sunlight pouring through apricot and green glass,
the catalpa's white blossoms tipping rain,
tufting mounds of lavender and sage,
a clean tablecloth topped with a blue glazed bowl,
mugs hung open on their hooks.

And if I could have come alive, I would have seen
that everything had a shape and a place
and was shining. But because I'd chosen,
in some early measured moment,
the world of things, rather than
the world of things' meanings,
I lived in disproportion.

I thought the purses had caught me in their maws.
I thought I'd be buried by the bone china.
How could I breathe in the fumes of our buying
and selling, our endless hungry plundering?
How could I proceed from that wound
of separateness, scab picked at
and bandaged in each of us?

We use it—our desperation—
to strangle our air. And the wound
unfolds as world, vibrating always
outward in its own reflections,
in vast acidic waters, where the burnt wash
and the harmed try to breathe
among our garbage
and discarded machines.

And now our imitation of life
hovers up, becomes more and more abstract.
Now it's the movement of things
we're trying to extract, the energetic dance.

As if we'd like to leave the living world
to our burning.

And So the Head Breaks Through

Walls shine with greenery,
roses crushed by our heels
glow red on the floor.

Grass rises happier for its hair.

—Fortunatus to Radegunde, Sixth-Century France

TORTUGA

In the deep of night, we were rowed across
a channel, a flat reflecting tendril of the sea.
We stared into the drifts of stars, folds
of dark water, and no one spoke.

Our guide was weary of being a guide,
tired of peeling himself away from his wife
and their yeasty bed of sleep
after a long day of hard work and low pay

to row people through miles of night
to what they may or may not be able to see.
He'd met so many who could not see.
And yet it was his job. He had children to feed.

He wearily, evenly rowed us across,
then hopped out, into the shallows,
holding the boat by a rope.
We took off our shoes and stepped into

water ankle-deep and skin-warm
and the ocean we understood then
was soft as a body, the ocean
was a body beating with stars.

Stars laced the lipping waves and glimmered
like chips of glass in the sand.
They dripped in glittering strands
over our ankles, across the pleated tops of our feet,

as we walked over that soft borderland
collapsing and the water swallowed
the marks we had made.
We walked through our memories,

our questions, until we forgot
why we were walking, until someone asked
What are these lights in the water?
And, just like that, her question made them real.

Plankton, our guide answered, *tiny plants
spawned to communicate with the moon.*
Then a great viridian creature
crawled out from the water.

For ages, she'd ridden the currents
with the others. She'd set off,
quick as a skiff, then threaded
the tides ever further, deeper,

arriving, finally, to give birth
on the same star-strewn sand,
at the same star-strewn moment
that she was born.

She lumbered up the dune,
chose her spot, blind, in a daze—
she had not eaten for days—
and began to dig.

Her broad flippers plunged and scooped
the sand—she was not made for land—
and in damp fists it dropped as she paddled back
to protect what her body had made.

She did not know if she would survive,
she did not wonder. We were the ones
who'd imagined surviving, who had walked
all that way holding our own shoes.

She dug until her death and it was in death
that the egging began—her body releasing
the slick, viscid, jelly-eyed moons
color of light before color

and they came from her
quickly and quickening, each a world
and a furtherance of the world,
as we in our wonder leaned closer,

kneeling in the sand like children.
Watching her work like this,
we saw the world we thought we lived in
had been much too small.

The sky was not a woven thing.
The night was not a tablecloth scattered with salt.
And our hands, which were wet
with flecks of ocean, secret tears

and secretions of boredom,
shone now with something shared.
Our toes hooked the sand and flashed once
their drying, dying stars.

And So the Head Breaks Through

The head breaks through
blood, hair and sinew to crown
darkly on a rhythm for a minute
in its own receding liquid, and then

air—do we ever recover
from the shock of it—roughing
us out to appendage?

How do we begin shoveling it in
to our lungs, how do we trust it
enough to swallow—this dry sea
swallowing us?

It happens in the tightthroat
threat of death and never ends.
Each of us stepping out
into our lives, surprised—

your limbs a spray of sparks,
my eyes fisted wide like a fish,
until some memory, recognition
thickens the limbs like a syrup,
solidifying the moment we're in.

HER

Do you remember
first recognizing your mother?

Shore in a tumult of light,
you knew her as you had always
known her—those elegant arms, her hands
like the waters raining your brow,
and her wound that would not
close. She tore herself out from it
into you—terroring
into hard air and hunger.

Your closed eyes
threading memory's tides
disclosed only the folded surface
of the blind, fish-fogged
and fluttering. Little wrinkled
mirror, little slough of the skin,
where did she end and you
begin?

And what of the joy-ache,
the shape you together made?

DUAL

So which of us is the beholder,
and which the beholden?

And why must we, the mirrored ones,
the ones with swollen waves in our hearts
and this quickening wind in our limbs,
step back again and again into the dual world?

Wouldn't you rather pass the world
through your body, through the opening
alveoli of your lungs and your eyes' far fathoms?
Wouldn't you rather remember being grass?

We grew together then, in tingling tufts
of nerves, and we smarted in our tips
and toughened in our roots, and we knew
the evening's gradual blues and red
coming fast from the future's body.

We knew the wound that wracked the back
of the mother's cupboards and rattled
in her hands, those mute utensils.

They were not lilies or fish
hooked by rings, not forms
for gloves cut from the skin of the lamb,
they were hands.

They came as leverage and flesh
stars, charged
to make and to mend.
They were hands.

GLYPH

Once we had names
we were born knowing.
Mine surfaced in me,
in the slow river of sleep.

I slept in its shapes, then I
lost it and now must live
lifetimes meeting it back.

The dogs at the gate will stop barking.
The snow on the ground will shine
coarse as sand and the day's conversation.

There will be smokestacks and steeples,
sun sparking on cinders,
and you will sleep, dreaming blood
on your tongue and the body you loved
and wore around you once,

wading eyeless through water,
stumbling through breathbeat
to a song. Did you feel those
tiny, ancient lives nipping
at your ankles? Did you fish them out
and call them sounds?

I was one of them—
minnow, crayfish, finned seed—
before you called my name and it
summoned me.

CIRCLE

Now I slip through the weave
of dune grass and chicory
into a scene . . .

children, sitting on the beach
listening as she tells a story. It seems
to be the story of birth

and its recurring impossibility
and the faith that makes its filaments
sing. You are one of the children

with her heart drumming wonder
into arms, knees, feet, her whole body
listening, or you want to be

but so far are only the wind—
the breath she breathes
through threads of grass

pressed between the warm ridged pads
of her thumbs—a whistling
you once as another

called to the tribe,
meaning, *Here I come.*

ONCE I WOKE ON THIS WISH

On a quilt-covered bed,
beside French doors open to the breeze,
grasses singing with the lisp and hush of timelessness.

I had fallen asleep reading,
my face spread flat on a spread
of people who were free.
They were beautiful.
They had beautiful white teeth.

And I knew I could turn the page
and there I'd be—bored and baubled
in a body that no longer belonged to me
but was a wand for something beyond me.

Then I awoke from that dream,
to this one. I turned this page,
and the wind it made was nearly wind,
and the page was nearly wing.

I could hear the live earth singing,
and I stepped out, into the greening.

As If Moving Spectral By

You have given me great verses on small tablets.
You can create honey in the wax . . .
by whose words you bind our heart.

—Fortunatus to Radegunde, Sixth-Century France

An Afterward

Marisol, who still lives with her parents in Marin County, is not me but may as well be. She has wanted to see. She has wanted always to live the right life—as if there were only one life, ultimately, for her.

And Jon? It seems Jon was simply waiting. He was waiting for his life to tell him what life would mean, and when he met Marisol, he felt it beginning to find a shape. The trinkets and antiques he moved among were no longer such compelling stories, they were no longer other lives that could envelop him. They were just things, and the people who had loved them had moved on, into other lives and other movements, other forms of use, and existences, he hoped, beyond use. Jon was beginning to feel there could be some movement in his life, like he could enter a stream, at last, beyond stillness, beyond the dust-gathering of fixity.

And Marisol was all movement, and she never had much to show for her work. She wrote for others' buying and selling and desire to outrun death with some new product. For the last few months, she had worked on an account for Dove—which once had been a bird that symbolized world peace and now was a line of body cleaning products. It was Marisol who had first thought to put real women in the ads. Real women in real underwear, in their real thighs and real breasts—on billboards and bus stops, laminated on the sides of trains. And moving quickly by—seeing them everywhere—seeing the money this would bring her, everywhere—Marisol wondered if this had been the right thing, after all, if finally it was worse to be selling real women to real women—as if a purchase should be the vehicle in which to behold yourself. Especially the purchase of a product made with phosphates that would only go on to poison the oceans.

Jon to her amid all this was like a fixed star. When he described a thing from the shop, she became as still as that thing. When he described for her the silver scarab bracelet with the chips of rubies for eyes, she imagined he was describing her own transformation.

You see, Jon and Marisol both wanted to become real. Marisol had become quickened motion and Jon had become the nostalgic stronghold of the physical, and both were realizing that they did not feel quite real, though neither really knew what they meant by that feeling.

Marisol, when she traveled, liked to look at home decorating magazines. She would be a half a mile up in the sky, arcing from L.A. to Chicago and staring hard into warmly lit rooms she told herself really existed, back in the world. She knew that the stylists had filled the room with extra knickknacks and bowls of fruit, but, still, the room itself existed—even the woman moving through its background—too fast for the camera's blink as if to say we all blur spectral through our lives—even that woman existed. She could solidify her edges and define her meaning there in that room of things. Marisol would devour these magazines cover to cover then buzz for a while with wanting. And today, while she buzzed like this, something new had happened. Her imagining had expanded to include Jon, in her rooms, and the things Jon would bring to her rooms—burled desks and jeweled brooches that they would pin like tiny surprises in the curtains.

Meanwhile Jon, knowing Marisol was in the air, looked up from the windows of his shop to the sky. The sky looked to him like a blank screen. Or it looked like something half-erased. He then looked back into his shop, at his sleeping cat, Archibald, and all of a sudden wished he could shrug off his shop like a garment. It had been cool once, if always a bit self-conscious, but now it was as if he was waking up—and feeling it as wool, as something tight-fitting, its pockets cluttered with junk. And while he stood there noting this, he felt himself releasing through the top of his head and saw himself far below standing in the doorway. Very still, his hands hanging pawlike at his sides. And he saw all around him the furniture and lamps and polished instruments, china and glass—how fragile it all seemed from this distance, but nothing, no object, was as fragile and rare as him—the bald spot on the top of his head just beginning, the vein twitching in his forearm—there was so much this body wanted, and who knew what kind of time there was. Jon kept going up and up. He was so small. And there were so many of these soft bodies moving about—so busily and bravely, it seemed—buzzing around in their metal pods, stepping through the doors of houses, putting bits of cooked root, and cooked meat, into their mouths. It was the grandest teeming tapestry.

And then he saw his parents. His mother in the kitchen fixing lunch and his father already eating his sandwich—bologna on a bun—sitting crouched at the table in front of the television, with the news on. The news flashed burning oil fields, flooding in the south. And his father chewed his sandwich. And the sandwich looked so small in his hands and his father looked so small before the news, which wormed out of the television and into his father's wrinkled brow and into his mother's nervous ways, and he saw for the first time his mother's rage, how it was barely contained in her frayed nerves, her reluctance to sit. He saw how his mother blamed his father, and how it ate at her like an ulcer, and how that had been the illness—her rage.

And in the slope of his father's shoulders, under the old plaid shirt he knew so well, Jon saw something like regret, remorse. But remorse embedded in the knowledge that he couldn't have known. That's right, isn't it? He couldn't have known how to live differently. He had done his best and would continue to do his best. He'd known a few women. He'd been a good husband and father and the house was almost paid for and they were going to rent an R.V. and take a week or two in Arizona. He could go around and around it, but he couldn't quite get to it, it seemed. This thing in him.

And Jon saw all of this and he ached for them and loved them— not like a man loves his children, which is a chilling and propulsive thing, but like a man loves a very dear memory that he knows will go on unfolding in its own world, its own dimension, while he sleeps. And so he loved them, he loved them each, and yet he saw that their lives were not his life. He saw that they had been staring so long at a television screen that they had not looked up in a long time. He saw that they had given him life but now they could not see his life.

Around this time, Marisol was half a mile above Chicago, where she and Jon had met. She had read all her magazines and so now was interrogating her hungers—for houses, for Jon and his body, for the promise of this friendship they had, and also for mercury glass lamps and cedar-lined armoires. She was thinking the perfect room for her would be a room in motion.

And she remembered one of her fantasies as a child—conjured up on long hot family drives to Mexico. Javier's smelly feet would be creeping toward her lap and Edith's baby body would be leaning against her. And she would put her cheek on the warm purring window and think she was stepping into a room. It was that easy. And it was a huge room with cloud-colored carpeting and long gossamer curtains, and in the center of the room was a white canopy bed. It was so spacious, she could dance around in it. She could jump on the bed and twirl and run while in the car she had to sit still, in her place, looking out the window and propping up the others. Sometimes she'd look up, stop to break up an argument between Edith and Javier, or to tell a joke or sing along with a song on the radio, then she'd go right back to that room. It was clean there, and large, and in the corner was a doll's house like no house she had ever seen. It was colorful and constructed of turrets and cupolas, balconies and staircases. And she could look into its many rooms and see that it would be her life.

*

I thought the wish was for a container: a book. But it was for a conveyer. Jon and Marisol's story leapt into an earlier story, of Radegunde and Fortunatus, which opened me into the story of my own life—a life of many wavelengths, many changes which kept on changing me. The true union of souls will spark both what is of the union, and beyond it. The true book will begin talking back in its own voice, I think.

Marisol laughed. This had been a good conversation. Today they had gotten right into it.

"My mom used to always tease me for staring into space," she told Jon. "But now I make my living staring into space."

Jon thought, Marisol has a way of talking that sounds like a perpetual ending. All her years in advertising had given her this penchant for "wrapping up."

But Jon sensed this perpetual ending was just a fear of ending, her fear that the conversation would have to end, that he would be the one to end it first.

"I know a few stories," Jon said, shyly.

"So do I," Marisol said.

But instead of telling one, or asking to hear one, which he knew would have been about her, and therefore about him, Jon became quiet. He didn't know what to say suddenly. It was like cleverness and stories were falling away, becoming just like props, like words.

"Do you ever wonder if we are just evolved and shifted versions of our parents?" Marisol asked after a while.

"I used to. But I was thinking today and something changed. I saw my parents like I was seeing them from a distance and I saw that they can't see my life. I feel suddenly like I'm becoming myself, I don't know, like my particular movements and idiosyncrasies will never be repeated."

"I think that is love," Marisol said. "To know that this person, and each moment with this person, could never be replaced."

NOTES

(p. xv) This quote is from *Stigmata: Escaping Texts* by French writer Hélène Cixous (Routledge Classics, 2005). The passage is part of an examination of the martial sensibility of the Bible, which privileges male heroes. How can human love fit in, Cixous asks, "amid the clash of arms, angers, incest crimes and punishment" and of which only a tiny portion, *Song of Songs*, "is reserved for indigenous love"?

"The Bibles never died," Cixous reminds us. "And they engendered most of the books we read. [But] there are a small number, the miracles, a handful of charming grains of sand in the desert of millennia. The secret guardians of the inestimable richness of being two different yet equal beings in terms of strengths and differences. Both, as much one as the other, equally mysterious."

(p. 15) The first "Fortunatus" I mention here is thanked by St. Paul in 1 Corinthians, verse 16: "I rejoice over the coming of Stephanas and Fortunatus and Achaicus, because they have supplied what was lacking on your part. For they have refreshed my spirit and yours. Therefore acknowledge such men."

Fortunatus was one of the most influential poets of his day, and Radegunde was a powerful abbess who was sainted after her death. Fortunatus composed many poems to Radegunde and also wrote her biography. One poem, "The Fall of Thuringia," is said to be co-authored by them and is written in Radegunde's voice. A few of her lines are echoed in my poems, especially those about her brother, "he who never gave a hard word." See Fortunatus's "Life of the Holy Radegund," translated by J. McNamara and J. Halborg, at <http://mv.mcmaster.ca/scriptorium/radegund.html> and *Sainted Women of the Dark Ages*, edited by Jo Ann McNamara and John E. Halborg with E. Gordon Whatley (Durham, NC: Duke University Press, 1992).

These excerpts from Fortunatus's letters and poems are my own hybrids of several available translations from the Latin. For translations of Fortunatus see *A Basket of Chestnuts*, translated by Geoffrey Cook (Rochester, NY: Cherry Valley, 1981); *Venantii Fortunati, Opera Poetica*, edited by Fridericus Leo (Berlin: Weidmann, 1881); and *Venantius Fortunatus: Personal and Political Poems* by Judith George (Liverpool: Liverpool University Press, 1995).

(p. 53) Orpheus is the quintessential poet, who in Greek myth charms the gods of the underworld with his lyre and is allowed to rescue his departed beloved, Eurydice. He can bring her back from the dead as long as he does not turn back to make sure she is following him.

(p. 75) In "Challah," the lines, "But you were never / happy then, not with me" were borrowed from the poet Jivin Misra.

(p. 91) Moriah is the name of the mountain where Abraham took Isaac to be sacrificed.

Thank You

To my parents, Cindy and Jim Webster, for giving me this amazing life, which I experience as lives within a life, times within time. To John McCarthy, superb editor and beloved partner. You are in everything I believe in, and this book would not exist without you. To Ted Morrissey, tremendous editor and publisher, for meeting this manuscript with respect and ferrying it into the world. To Richard Fammerée, for inspiring the writing of these poems, and for teaching me to live in time more fully and lovingly. To Adèle Fammerée, who began as a voice and arrived as my greatest blessing, our daughter. To my brother, Douglas Webster, who was my first best friend and reason for writing (see "Wish"). To my essential readers—Josie Raney, Adam Nicholson and Pamm Collebrusco— who gave their care and close attention. To Daniel Johnson, who sent me the blank book that became this. To Stanzi Vaubel, who helps me to listen more closely. To my students, who inspire me and give me hope. And to my friends who share this ever-evolving soul-space: Jullianna Nelson, Lucy Anderton, Stephanie Smith, Ric Edinberg, Rachael Gates Bergan, Karen Geiger-Behm, Kristina Findlay Goel, Tom and Mary Ellen Jackson, David Pelzer, Carrie Ingrisano, Michael Simons, Lauren Levato Coyne, Bhikshuni Weisbrot, Jesse Lichtenstein, Ariel Barbick, Vanessa Filley-Zises, David Lagerman, Meghan O'Rourke, Eula Biss . . . and the list expands. Thank you.

About the Author

Rachel Jamison Webster grew up in Madison, Ohio, on Lake Erie and now lives in Evanston, Illinois, where she teaches at Northwestern University. She is the author of *September* (Northwestern University Press, 2013), and two chapbooks, *The Blue Grotto* and *Leaving Phoebe*, both from Dancing Girl Press. For several years, she designed and taught writing workshops for urban youth, helping to develop Words 37 with Chicago's First Lady Maggie Daley and co-editing two anthologies of writing by young Chicagoans, *Alchemy* (2001) and *Paper Atrium* (2005).

Rachel holds an M.F.A. from the Warren Wilson Program for Writers. She has won awards from the Academy of American Poets, The American Association of University Women and The Poetry Center of Chicago. Her poems and essays have been published in many anthologies and journals, including *Poetry*, *Tin House*, *Narrative*, *The Paris Review* and *Labor Day: Birth Stories from Today's Best Women Writers* (FSG, 2014). Rachel is also the editor of the online anthology of international poetry, universeofpoetry.com. You can read more about her at racheljamisonwebster.com.

Photo by Richard Fammerée

Quiddity Interview with the Author

This interview appeared in *Quiddity* international literary journal, issue 8.1, and is reprinted with permission.

In The Endless Unbegun *you tell an interconnected story through different forms and timelines, creating a book that is as anachronistic as it is truthful. Can you speak to how this combination of forms, poetry and prose, and your perception and portrayal of narrative throughout this project echo your other work, especially in relation to time, both secular and sacred?*

Well, poetry is always about time, in both its subject and its repetition of sounds. My first book, *September*, stems primarily from the lyric impulse—an intense feeling that moves through the body, and moves through the poem in a form of rhythm. It's how the emotion is created in the body of the reader, through the rhythm of the word. I think of poetry as a physical, musical impulse, still very connected to its roots as an oral art form.

And although there is definitely a sonic sense in *The Endless Unbegun*, this book is driven more by narrative. It is essentially a set of interlinked stories about people who meet as different selves, in different lifetimes. I saw *The Endless Unbegun* almost as a series of spaces that we walk into—labyrinthine, repetitive spaces that are increasingly free of persona and specifics. It starts with a prose narrative about Jon and Marisol, who live in our time at the beginning of the twenty-first century. Then, it shifts into the voice of Radegunde, who was an earlier vessel, an Abbess who lived in sixth-century Gaul. In the book, Radegunde is both this historical figure and potentially me, the speaker. The work overtly plays with mergers of voice and of self. And so by the time the reader arrives at the center of the book, the speaker feels almost selfless, not in an altruistic way, but in the sense that I can't really locate the voice as me or as any other character. It is a shared voice of intuition, ideally.

And I guess this is how I think of stories, as layers of awareness, constructions we live through and then break out of. I think poets live and write stories in order to transcend them.

Can you say more about this philosophy of narrative? Is it dismissive of stories?

I guess I think that the deepest work happens outside of any narrative, in something more like inspiration, or meditation. Our stories are creations. We tell stories about who we are or who we were in order to know ourselves, but there's always the tinge of artifice. And pure poetry can be utterance that is not as invested in that artifice. And so I think of these as different wavelengths, and it seems that in order to function in the world—and for me to function as an artist—we have to learn how to live on many different wavelengths.

I love the vehicle of story, but I also love the moment when you feel like you've slipped outside of story, outside of your persona, outside of your name, and could be almost any self, at any point in time. Walt Whitman, my first favorite poet, wrote, "I contain multitudes." We all do. If we plumb the imagination, and we plumb our dreams, and we develop that empathic function that is so special about being human, then we realize that there are all kinds of "others" in us.

How did this book begin?

It started in almost a novella form about Jon and Marisol, in the present time. Their wish is to meet, to meet a partner in a space that transcends persona, transcends the idea of relating to someone almost as an object, a means to an end. They don't necessarily know how to verbalize it, but that is their secret hope. It's a hope for a love that has its own life, that has an inevitability about it, the spark of the soul, I could say. And their hope began to mirror my own hope—for a book which also had its own soul and propulsion, that would transform me in its making, as any real love does.

There's a book by the theologian Martin Buber called *I and Thou*. I realize that the ideas in his book really influenced *The Endless Unbegun*. One of Buber's central claims is that in any situation we have the opportunity to meet someone as an *I-It* or an *I-Thou*. In the *I-It* relationship the other is a means to an end. She is going to help me get a promotion or she is going to make me look good as my girlfriend, etc. It is another being related to basically as an object.

The other way of encounter that Buber writes about is the *I-Thou* relationship, which is the self meeting the holiness of another, or the wholeness of another. This is what yogis mean when they say, "Namaste," the holiness in me bows to the holiness in you. This reverence for another's wholeness creates a completely different kind of relationship. It is not easy because it has in it the very seed of transformation. If two people really meet as equals, they are going to be changed. Ultimately, those were the questions that I was asking and working with when I was writing *The Endless Unbegun*.

You mentioned how the narrative drops from the modern world into a deeper world through the inhabitance of different voices, creating these interior poems. Would you elaborate on how you channeled those voices and what it was like to inhabit those voices?

Well, the novella opened into poems. The poems, which were from my own life, opened into poems about these characters who lived in the Dark Ages, maybe because I suspect that we are living at the beginning of another Dark Age. These characters, who lived in sixth-century France, were real figures named Radegunde and Venantius Fortunatus. When Radegunde was a girl, she was kidnapped from her homeland by Clotaire, King of the Franks. He killed everyone in her family, plundered her kingdom, then took her as his wife by force. She refused that marriage and became a holy woman, and ended up establishing an abbey for women—somehow with Clotaire's support. After creating this safe house for other women, she became a leader and a writer. She wrote to kings, bishops, princes, and people in power, and shared her unique perspective as she tried to create peace and influence history.

Her best friend was a troubadour, who was actually the most well-known poet of his day: Venantius Fortunatus. He wrote many poems and letters to Radegunde, and they had a friendship of equals. It seems to be that they couldn't have had a physical, romantic relationship then because she was married to God as a nun, and he was married to his work. Because he was a public poet, he had to be part marketer and part flatterer. But he was a genuinely talented person.

I want to go a little deeper into myth and religious themes. You mentioned that Radegunde was married to God as a nun. And that she and Fortunatus had this relationship back and forth over letters. Their voices and their writings contain lots of religious references. Even in your own work, The Endless Unbegun *and* September, *you use many Jewish and Christian references and often call upon religious feelings. Can you speak to how you and your writing are influenced by the religious voice, and what do you hope to accomplish by its incantation on the page?*

That's a great question. I think I was a very secular writer and thinker, and then my life shifted and I had to acknowledge that the metaphysical is centrally important to me. To me, this process feels like an adventure of consciousness to see further all the time.

Blind faith doesn't actually work for me, and neither does any orthodox or dogmatic view. I am not someone who can receive tenets whole and just believe them. But my own life has had a shapeliness to it, even a magic to it. I have a sense of wonder about how things unfold, and I see patterns in life's development and repetitions, and I believe in forces beyond us. The way I have examined my life and lived my life has made me a spiritual person. I believe in a pattern that is more than we can see, that this world offers shimmering glimpses of. This must be destruction and creation, death and life, which is life, in ever more complex or elegant arrangements. But I do believe that there is meaning to all of this. I believe that our participation really matters, and we can develop a sense of humility, a respect for ourselves and for what is beyond us, and a generative sense of wonder. That is my belief system.

I am also very aware of how belief systems form our world. Facts can be interpreted any which way, and whether we acknowledge it or not, they are always interpreted along accepted lines of story and myth. Perception is sifted through a shape people can agree upon. So we have dominant paradigms and also all of these shadow shapes in our culture, and I think Christianity is still a central underlying story. The way this story is told still informs the shape in which so many things are understood—sacrifice and martyrdom and the rise of the individual hero, who is male. So I guess I am endlessly interested in examining the way the stories we tell ourselves shape our understanding of everything.

Were you raised in a Christian household?

I was not raised in a traditional religious household, but I was raised in this country, in Protestantism, close to nature, and spirituality was always important to me. I have studied many other spiritual texts like the *Bhagavad Gita*, the *Yoga Sutras of Patanjali*, the *Upanishads*, which also shape a sense of self, but I have to acknowledge the Judeo-Christian framework of this culture.

And the problem is, if you really study Judeo-Christian patterning, there isn't quite enough there for women. It's not equal. There are all these female sources of understanding and spiritual wisdom that are completely left out of canonical spiritual texts. And natural sources, learning from the Earth, learning from our observations of nature, are other areas that tend to be either ignored or maligned. And this becomes a real conundrum for a woman who feels sincerely spiritual. The Eastern paths are very rich, and I love the idea of mindfulness, but those texts are also male. So, what do you do when that is the case?

Throughout my book, there is actually a distrust of texts. All the speakers, at some point, call out books as being limited. That was a very conscious choice. The written word has done more than any other innovation to advance our consciousness as humans, but it has also done great harm to Earth-centered cultures, to female wisdom, to alternate ways of knowing and finding meaning.

So how much would you say The Endless Unbegun *speaks to equality and gender?*

Well, most of these poems are grappling with meaning from a female point of view, from the point of view of someone who feels connected to nature and also believes in the spiritual unfolding within each precious life. For instance, there is a poem in here called "Moriah" [pp. 91-3], and it is the retelling of the story of Abraham and Isaac, imagining what it would have been like for Sarah to watch that near-murder unfold. She rages, she screams into wind, and her scream is drowned out and rendered impotent. But she reminds us, "That was the miracle: being a body." She doesn't need more of a miracle than that. I wanted to remind us of the miraculous nature of being here, on earth, in a body, in a life. Not to mention the miraculous nature of creating life through the body, which is the wonder that women get to experience. I actually think that male-based religions probably arose to compensate for the female's amazing reproductive power. There's also a poem here called "Tortuga" [p. 101], which is about watching a giant sea turtle give birth, releasing her lucent eggs in the sand. I saw this once, and it was an amazing experience, a timeless wonder that I will never forget.

So, this book follows a different set of assumptions—that it *is* spiritual work to notice where we are on Earth, in nature and in our bodies.

Let's acknowledge that some of the early religious origin stories, in early African cultures and Native American cultures, were about Mother Earth—the mother as creator—and that the female was the creator and giver of life. So, is it not only counterintuitive but also unhealthy to not have a sense of equality when combining art with the spiritual when making a worldview?

That is such a good question and point. Thank you! I think that is the hope, and the book declares itself as a wish for that equality between male and female, physical and spiritual. As I understand it, Native Americans had a sophisticated and metaphorical way of seeing the world in which everything that they lived or saw in nature was a potential teacher, a potential message delivered from the Spirit, just for them and their people. I love living that way. That is the path that really feeds my poetry and life. And their ancient story that Earth is a turtle moving through space fits with this poem "Tortuga," and the sense that the Earth is continually giving birth to itself, that we are part of that continual cycle of death and renewal.

That sounds very Buddhist. Is there any Eastern sensibility here?

Well, yes! The entire book is predicated on the idea of reincarnation, and I keep making mention of coming back and coming back and meeting again in different forms. I have a very nonliteral relationship to this idea of reincarnation. I don't think it could be a direct equation, and yet the cycling of souls makes sense to me. If you look at nature, everything returns. If we are energetic beings, and now we can prove that we are, of course our energies would return in some way. So, the book takes the idea of reincarnation as a metaphor, and the idea of meeting someone and loving someone so you feel like you remember them.

For me, that feeling probably began with the birth of my brother when we were little. It was like I was waiting for him to be born. Then, there he was, so much like I had pictured him! There is a child who comes later in *The Endless Unbegun*, and that is my daughter, and I felt the same way about her. I think that could just be love, though. When you love people in the *I-Thou* relationship, you can't imagine not ever having loved them. It is like love has dropped you through time; you've always loved each other and will always love each other. So, it is almost impossible not to see this person in your past and your future. That is when these metaphors, these stories and relationships that we live, become really meaningful and interesting.

What you have described to me is very conceptual, very historical, but stylistically speaking, on a page-by-page basis, how do you actually frame all these ideas of the female and reincarnation in a way that accurately imparts their meaning across the page, and hopefully across time?

In this book, it is through images as much as anything. Lots of water, lots of boats, and then very loosely implied story that has to do with near union, near union, union, near union, and then the result of a union in which both parties are transformed. There's a poem on a boat traversing waters, called "Bardo" [pp. 69-70], which is the space between lives, the Buddhists believe. So I think the reader experiences the book as, "Uh-oh, suddenly I'm in another life, I'm in another iteration, meeting again or traveling again." Also, there is the child's voice that interrupted this book as I was writing it. That, to me, metaphorically symbolizes the fruits of a union. When two full consciousnesses come together, then they are going to lead to a third consciousness. Maybe they will lead to an actual child, maybe to a book, but, no matter what, there is going to be some new creation out of full, soulful meeting.

The book as a creation was beyond me like this. And so I needed time, distance, and a really good editor's help. First, it was just a sprawling book of intuitive prose. Then I whittled it down into poems, which took years. A lot of the themes kept returning, like boats and water, but it felt like a lot for a reader to navigate and for me to frame in an objective way. So, more than any other project I have done, I actually needed confirmation from a couple of excellent readers that the book did not just exist as a subconscious web of associations. I don't think it's going to be an easy book, but I do believe in its intuitive logic. And if you have an appreciation of the spiritual, of guidance, of intuition, and of natural life, then you should be able to understand it. The reader should be able to come away with his or her own realizations and interpretations. That is my hope, anyway!

Thank you, Rachel. Is there anything else you would like to add to how space and time, spiritual or secular inhabit the nature of your poetry, or of The Endless Unbegun?

I guess I just want to thank you for the nature of these questions. I love poetry for helping us to trust this metaphorical space as a source of real meaning. Poetry is, for me, the spiritual and meta-phorical freed of dogma. We get to live poems, which means we don't just have to receive belief systems. We get to wake up to our own lives and relationships and trust that they have import that is real, within us and beyond us—and always evolving.

A Note on the Type

The text of the book is set in Adobe's version of Garamond, styled after a type developed by punch-cutter Claude Garamont (circa 1480-1561). There are several typefaces called Garamond that vary slightly from Garamont's original design. The titles are set in Book Antiqua, a typeface modeled after the Palatino typeface, designed by master calligrapher Giambattista Palatino in sixteenth-century Italy.